W9-AUE-495
BLAINE MN 55434 2398
REMOVED FROM
ANOKA COUNTY LIBRARY
COLLECTION

THE PRINCE
AND
THE PRINCESS

MARIANNA MAYER is one of the country's foremost storytellers of fairy tales, folktales, and myths. She is the author of over two dozen books for young readers, with over one-half million copies in print. Her books include *My First Book of Nursery Tales,* illustrated by William Joyce; *A Boy, a Dog, a Frog and a Friend* with Mercer Mayer; and *The Brambleberrys®* animal books illustrated by Caldecott winner Gerald McDermott. Her fairy tales include *Beauty and the Beast,* illustrated by Mercer Mayer; *The Unicorn and the Lake,* illustrated by Michael Hague; *The Ugly Duckling,* illustrated by Thomas Locker; and most recently *The Twelve Dancing Princesses,* illustrated by K.Y. Craft. In addition, she has written THE SORCERER'S APPRENTICE, illustrated by David Wiesner, another book in her continuing series for Bantam Books.

JACQUELINE ROGERS's work has appeared both on the cover of and as text illustration for a number of books for young readers, most notably the *Blossom* family series for Delacorte Press. She lives with her husband and baby daughter in Spencertown, New York.

THE PRINCE AND THE PRINCESS

A Bohemian Fairy Tale

by

MARIANNA MAYER

with illustrations by

JACQUELINE ROGERS

A BANTAM SKYLARK BOOK®

NEW YORK • TORONTO • LONDON • SYDNEY • AUCKLAND

For Emma Tillinger

M.M.

To Michael

J.R.

THE PRINCE AND THE PRINCESS
A Bantam Skylark Book / November 1989
Skylark Books is a registered trademark of Bantam Books, a division of Bantam Doubleday Dell Publishing Group, Inc. Registered in U.S. Patent and Trademark Office and elsewhere.
All rights reserved.
Text copyright © 1989 by Marianna Mayer.
Illustrations copyright © 1989 by Jacqueline Rogers.
Book design by Debby Jay.

Library of Congress Catalog Card Number: 89-37435

No part of this book may be reproduced or transmitted in any form or by any means, electronic or mechanical, including photocopying, recording, or by any information storage and retrieval system, without permission in writing from the publisher.
For information address: Bantam Books.

ISBN 0-553-05843-6

Published simultaneously in the United States and Canada

Bantam Books are published by Bantam Books, a division of Bantam Doubleday Dell Publishing Group, Inc. Its trademark, consisting of the words "Bantam Books" and the portrayal of a rooster, is Registered in U.S. Patent and Trademark Office and in other countries. Marca Registrada. Bantam Books, 666 Fifth Avenue, New York, New York 10103.

PRINTED IN THE UNITED STATES OF AMERICA

WAK 0 9 8 7 6 5 4 3 2 1

Preface

DURING the nineteenth century in many European countries folktales and fairy tales enjoyed a revival of great interest. The Bohemian tale *The Prince and the Princess* was no exception, and under the title *Long, Broad, and Quickeye* it, too, gained a wide and popular audience. Largely owing to that revival, there are today a number of versions, and as with many folk and fairy tales of long ago, there is no single author to credit and no original text to declare as *the definitive* source.

Nonetheless, research has made plain that many of the story elements have their roots in the pagan beliefs of the Slavic people who first settled in central Europe in the former kingdom of Bohemia, during the fifth century A.D. What remains of their early mythology, supplemented by old traditions, still lives on among the people in the form of legends and folktales. Indeed, their legends are richly imaginative and romantic while retaining strong ties to the ancient pagan myths.

A prime example is the Bohemian belief that the soul or spirit is a being quite distinct from the body, which it is free to leave even during life. There are in fact many stories similar to *The Prince and the Princess* that describe a human soul leaving the body to dwell elsewhere for a period of time. The spirit or soul might choose to inhabit a tree or take the shape of a dove, flying free in the world until such time as it chose to return and dwell again within its original human form.

The wild Forest of Lost Souls, another element in our story, is reminiscent of the powerful Bohemian superstition that all forests and groves are imbued with mystery and inhabited by strange beings endowed with supernatural abilities. In fact, it wasn't until the reign of Břetislav II in 1092 that the groves, held in high honor throughout Bohemia, were finally cut down and burned in order to encourage the people to embrace Christianity.

All such elements remind us of the wealth of poetic imagination inherent in what once must have been a compelling Slavic mythology. Too frequently the ancient records are scanty and fragmented, but the national tales, preserved to this day, remain the last resting place for the common folk beliefs of a time otherwise lost to us.

It was this author's task to create a fresh tale, motivated by these fragments but not rigidly based on material of the past. Instead, this story is an original tale, using old tradition as its source of inspiration. For this reason, *The Prince and the Princess* should be read not as a work of scholarship or adaptation, but as a work of pure imagination.

MARIANNA MAYER

Chapter One

IN A land far away, a long time ago, autumn had set in. The green of summer faded, changing leaves to yellow-orange, scarlet, and brown. Each golden afternoon turned cold by nightfall, when chilly winds blew in from the north, bringing a promise of winter.

At twilight as the fleeting light cast long gray shadows, an old king sat upon his throne, lost in thought. Gazing out the castle windows past the vast domain spreading before him, he shivered. Drawing his royal robes still closer, the king turned back to look at his son.

The young prince sat nearby, arms folded, legs crossed, patiently waiting for his father to resume

speaking. They had been discussing the king's fondest subject of late—the prince's future, which naturally included the future of the kingdom.

At last the king said, "Someday you'll be ruler of this land. Already my hair is streaked with gray, my steps are slow, and each passing day I grow more weary. Soon death will beckon like an old friend and I'll leave this life to follow."

The king did not fear death, for he had lived with honor and his deeds caused him no shame. Yet, while he lived, he wished to see his son marry.

Indeed, it was his dearest wish; only then did the king feel he would rest easy.

"Surely," continued the father, "there is some fine young maiden you might marry. It's time you chose a wife. The sooner you're wed, the happier I'll be."

The prince smiled and shook his head, saying, "Father, surely it will be many years before the ruling of the kingdom will pass to me. But just the same, believe me, I'd gladly marry if there were a maiden that I loved. As yet she has not crossed my path, but I'll find her. Sometimes in my dreams I've seen her, and I know one day we'll meet."

The king, who had been listening carefully, now drew from a wooden chest a key of gold. Placing it in his son's hand, he said, "Go then to the far side of the castle to the round stone tower. Climb the stairs to the very top and there you'll find a locked room. This key will open the lock. Perhaps what you discover there will help you."

Though the prince had never been in the tower and could not imagine what he might find, he did as his father asked. Once inside, he found a spiral staircase that led him up to a heavy black oak door cleverly carved to look like foliage—clusters of ivy and tendrils of clematis covered its surface and entwined the gilt handle and latch. Looking at it, the prince imagined that behind such a door anything might be waiting.

Intrigued, he fitted the key to the lock; it turned with difficulty, but opened at last. One rusty hinge cracked and broke as he pushed the door open. And then, suddenly, he was inside a magnificent circular room.

But it was unlike any room he had ever seen before, for it appeared as nothing so much as a wondrous forest glade in the land of enchantment. He took a step and saw he walked upon not a carpet but a lawn of closely cropped meadow grass here and there scattered with delicate wildflowers of palest blue and white. Overhead a ceiling of heavenly stars, small and sparkling, were flung upon a moonlit sky of iridescent blue. The surrounding walls were so shadowy and indistinct as to seem invisible, and the twelve tall stained-glass windows set into the walls in frames of gold looked as if they were suspended in thin air.

Through the colored glass the last rays of afternoon light streamed in, causing a myriad of rich hues to glow and shimmer with dazzling vibrancy. But radiant color was not all, for each glass panel held an exquisite, life-size likeness of a princess, and beneath each frame was a gold nameplate. The Princess Marina, The Princess Regina, The Princess Estansa, and so on, each princess more beautiful than the last.

"And so my father has sent me here to choose a bride from among these royal beauties," thought the prince. "Indeed, if a man were to travel the world over, he would not find more beautiful princesses." Pausing, he wondered, "Why is it then that I cannot choose?"

And then, as the prince studied the images, the figures began to make a startling change. Slowly, almost imperceptibly, the figures grew more and more real, until finally the images seemed like mirrors or reflections of living, breathing girls. What's more, each lovely princess suddenly looked directly at him and smiled. "In a moment," he thought, "they will step from the glass and speak."

Astonished, he turned to look again at each and every one. It was then that he caught sight of another window. He had missed it at first, and no wonder, for the last window, the thirteenth, was covered in a black drape. Without hesitating he went forward and pulled away the covering. The drape fell to the floor, revealing the last princess.

Eagerly he looked at her, and as he stared a sense of recognition spread over him like a great and powerful sea. Here was the princess he had dreamed of.

He must know her name. Tearing his eyes away, he searched beneath the frame for the nameplate. It had been removed. Looking back at her he felt his heart sink, for he saw what he had missed in the first excitement of recognizing her. Unlike the others, her image had not come to life. Indeed, her

eyes were closed. Everything—her pale white skin, her sad expression, the broken lilies at her feet—indicated that this maiden no longer lived.

But that could not be true, he told himself. There must be some other explanation. He must find the answer to this mystery. And in the silence of the tower, he spoke out, "This maiden, if she will have me, shall be my bride. I swear on my life, if I should live to be one hundred, I'll love no other."

No sooner did he speak this vow than the other princesses all together shuddered and breathed a sigh for him. There was a rumble of thunder. All at once the sky grew dark, and outside rain began to fall. A tear—or was it just a raindrop?—streaked down the nameless princess's cheek. There was a crack of lightning and for an instant the sky lit up. Suddenly, the twelve pretty princesses resumed their lifeless form. Still lovely, they were once again nothing more than stained-glass images.

The prince left the tower and returned to his father to tell him what had taken place. The old king listened, but he grew worried when his son repeated the vow he had made.

Sadly the king shook his head, saying, "You've chosen the impossible, my son. You should never have uncovered that hidden panel. The maiden you have vowed to love is the princess of the Iron Castle. In choosing her, you'll be hurled from the sure and safe road of life to follow a perilous destiny.

"You see, my son, some time ago the princess fell victim to a most powerful and wicked sorcerer. When she refused to marry him, he sought revenge against her. One night, while those in the castle slept, he cast an evil spell. Now the princess and her subjects are under the sorcerer's power, for he has turned them all to stone. Make no mistake, you'll not be the first brave young man to try to free her. Indeed, many have attempted it, but all have met the same fate—they, too, have been turned to stone.

"Nevertheless, your vow cannot be broken. You have given your solemn word, and regardless of my warning, I see that your mind and heart are made up. Go then, risk your fate for love of this poor maiden. I only pray that one day you will return unharmed."

Chapter Two

AT SUNRISE the next morning the prince was ready to start. Fog hung heavy, the leaves on the trees were glistening, and each blade of grass was silver with cold morning dew. Everything was still and silent as father and son said farewell. There were last minute instructions and hasty words of caution, but at last the prince mounted his sturdy gray horse and went riding off into the mist. His father watched as the fog opened reluctantly before horse and rider and then closed ominously, until all too quickly the prince was lost from view.

"Mind you stay north," his father had warned. "Take care that the old forest called the Forest of

Lost Souls doesn't make you its captive. Though you must pass through it, remember, few find their way out once they're inside."

At first the road was smooth enough; the fog began to lift, but the weather stayed damp and dreary much of the time. Days of riding brought the prince far from familiar paths till he was fast approaching the edge of the old forest. He could not go round it—the forest was too wide for that. He must take his chances and travel through.

But the dense gloom of the forest ahead gave him a strong sense of foreboding, for the Forest of Lost Souls was an eerie place. The trees that grew there did not like strangers very much and they were fond of playing tricks on travelers.

Once inside, the prince sensed the trees were whispering to one another, passing news or plots in a language beyond his understanding. The branches swayed and bent, reaching out even without a wind to stir them. As he advanced, the trees moved to surround him. Very shortly, he felt trapped. The broad path he had followed into the wood vanished. Narrow tracks crisscrossed here and there, shifting and changing till very quickly he was utterly lost. There was no sign of life as he wandered. He saw no bird or other animal, but in the distance, sometimes near, sometimes far, the silence was broken by the repeated cawing of unseen birds. Their plaintive calls were ever anxious and disturbing and underscored his growing sense of desolation.

The prince rode slowly on, his horse picking carefully over thick roots and thorny branches. One winding path after another led deeper and deeper into the unfriendly forest. He discovered dark valleys and murky streams, but never a sign of a way out.

A long night spent on the damp ground left him sleepless. At dawn, weary if still resolute, he rose and mounted his horse. But the tall trees shut out the sun, making it impossible to judge which direction might lead north or south, east or west.

Despairing and thoroughly confused, the prince dismounted to walk beside his horse. Suddenly he stopped. There was a sound, or so he thought, but it seemed to come from very far off, down the valley and farther back in the forest. He turned round and listened. His horse pricked up its ears and listened too. Soon there could be no doubt: someone was calling or singing. Then quite clearly there was a deep voice singing carelessly, but it sounded like nothing so much as a lot of nonsense:

"Hell-lo! Merry-lo! Ring ding a lo!
Forest high, forest low! Tall's my name and I wander here, there, everywhere
Up, down, all around!
High, low, don't you know!
Hell-lo! Merry-lo! Ring a ding a dell-lo!"

Full of hope, the prince called out, "Hello, there! Can you hear me?"

Just then the voice rose up loud and clear and ever so much closer. "And hello to you, sir! Tall's my name, sir. At your service."

The prince stood quite still as if in a trance. The wind blew through the trees. The leaves rustled with the breeze and softly whispered. There, behind a bramble bush, stood the fellow. He wore a peaked green hat with a long yellow feather stuck in the band. With a hop and a bounce, he was fully in view. He was too tall and skinny for an ordinary man, which naturally was the reason for his name. He strode forward in great big brown boots the size of buckets, took off his hat, and made a low, sweeping bow. He had a blue jacket somewhat tattered at the elbows and at the edges of his too short sleeves. He was clean-shaven and his bright twinkling eyes were at least as blue as his jacket, while his breeches were as red as a ripe red apple.

"How do you do?" said the prince at last.

"Well enough, sir. Thank you," Tall answered. Then the stranger paused. His eyes full of curiosity, he appeared quite content to wait and stare until the prince could collect his thoughts to speak again.

"I wonder," inquired the prince, after some moments passed in silence. "Can you tell me exactly where I am?"

"Why, sir! You're in the heart of the Forest of Lost Souls. The place we poor souls find when all else is lost. Those who have nowhere else to go and are of no use to anybody wander here. Can it be that you're not one of us?"

"I suppose I'm not," said the prince. "But days ago I left family and homeland behind to travel through this confounded forest in order to reach the Iron Castle that stands on the other side."

"Hush, sir! If you'll pardon me for saying, we must not speak ill of the forest or the trees will surely take offense. But, yes, I see . . . yours is another matter altogether," said Tall, thoughtfully. "Well then, you might say you've given up what you *had* in order to find what you *don't have*!"

In spite of his plight the prince had to laugh. "I suppose you're right," he said.

"Oh, sir! In that case, I beg you to take me into your service. You won't regret it, I promise you. Should you need anything, just say the word and I'll fetch it for you. A bird's nest perhaps? Look here, sir! I can have it for you in a jiffy."

Before the prince had a chance to reply, the eager fellow began to grow even taller. He stretched longer and longer until he was able to reach the tallest treetops. From that awesome height it was a simple matter to pluck a bird's nest from the nearest branch. Immediately, Tall shrank down to his usual size and thrust the empty nest into the prince's hand.

The young man hardly knew what to say. "Well, this is very fine indeed," said the prince without much conviction. "But I have little need of bird's nests at the moment. Now, if you could help me find the way out of here, I would gladly take you into my service."

"Just a minute and I'll see," said Tall as he began once again to stretch and stretch, higher and higher, until he was even taller than the tallest trees in the forest. Looking first one way and then

another, he shouted back down to the prince, "We must go this way, if we are to get out."

In another instant Tall had reduced in size, and with sudden determination he marched forward, leaving the prince to chase after him.

"Tell me, Tall," said the prince, after he finally had a minute or two to catch up. "If you knew all along how to find a route out of the forest, why haven't you tried to leave it before now?"

"Why, sir!" remarked Tall, quite astonished. "Since I was *lost* before I came to the forest, I've had no thought to leave it."

Now, the prince didn't understand this reasoning at all, but just then he didn't see any point in pursuing the matter. After all, up ahead there was no clear way out. However, Tall appeared to know exactly where he was headed. So the prince decided he had little choice; he must follow his newfound guide and hope for the best.

Chapter Three

WHEN, in a little while, the dense forest began to thin, Tall paused and turned back to the prince. "Sir, here comes a friend of mine. Please say you'll take him into your service," begged Tall. "If you refuse, he'll have to stay behind—lost as I was before I found you."

The prince did not know how to answer. In truth, he could not see how taking another lost soul into his service would help him rescue the princess. Instead, he said, "We shall see, my friend. Please call to him, so that I may meet the fellow and have a chance to consider the matter."

"Oh, thank you, sir! You won't regret it. But my friend is a long way off. Wait a moment and I'll fetch him."

Tall stretched until his head disappeared into the clouds above. He took two impossibly long strides, picked up his friend, and returned to set him before the prince.

The stranger grinned broadly and bowed. Unlike Tall, he was rather short in stature, but he was enormously large in other ways. In fact, his shape could only be described as big and round. Imagine a huge round ball and you have some idea of the shape of this cheerful fellow. He wore a voluminous scarlet cape and rather worn brown breeches, and tiny orange slippers covered his surprisingly small feet.

"At your service, your worship! Large is my name and you have my word that I am ever so willing and able to serve you. Only let me come along and I will strive to prove it," said the stout fellow, bowing gracefully.

The prince looked from Large to Tall and back again. What an amazing pair they made! "Well, Large," said the prince, "if I agree, what is it that you can do?"

"Your lordship! I can make myself as wide as you please. Would you care to see?"

"Certainly," said the prince. But he didn't know what he was agreeing to, for suddenly Large began

to swell like the inflatable balloon he resembled.

"Run away!" shouted Tall. "*Run away! Run away!*"

Now, the prince was a hero, make no mistake, and he did not think running away was precisely heroic. But, at the same time, he was no fool. So when he saw Tall flying for his life, he thought he had better do the same and ask questions later.

Indeed, it was just as well. Large grew and grew, until he had grown *so big* and *so round* that he covered a good deal of the available area and in the process nearly knocked the prince down. When the tremendous fellow stopped growing, he abruptly exhaled like a balloon letting out air, causing the trees to bend backward from the mighty force. Finally Large resumed his original shape, thereby allowing everyone else to sigh with relief.

"I'm not accustomed to running from my friends," said the prince as he came forward. "Well, I can't imagine what use your particular talent might provide. But as you and Tall seem determined to join me, I can only say I'm happy to accept."

In high spirits the prince and his two companions hastened through the dark forest, until, in late afternoon, they met another man. The prince was immediately struck by the sight of him, for the stranger had tied around his head a ragged blindfold to cover his eyes. To be sure, in other ways he was quite ordinary, if a bit shabby. He wore a tattered green velvet frock coat that reached to the tops of his knees, faded blue breeches, and high laced boots.

Tall and Large did not seem a bit taken aback when they saw him. Indeed, they greeted the stranger as though he was familiar to them.

"Sir," said Tall. "This is Sure-eyes. Please say he can come along with us. There has never been a finer gentleman, and he could be useful to you."

"Very well," said the prince, resigned not to argue. "But why are his eyes covered? Unless we agree to lead him, he shall never find his way anywhere."

"Excuse me, my lord," interrupted Sure-eyes. "Here you are mistaken. It is just the opposite. It's because I see *far too well* that I wear a blindfold. I can see through any object . . . even a man's mind. Such a skill can prove unwelcome . . . it has made an outcast of me.

"But, my vision does have its advantages. If you wish, I can give you a demonstration."

"By all means," said the prince, not knowing what to expect next.

Sure-eyes let the ragged band fall from his eyes. Quickly turning, he set his gaze upon a boulder some distance from where they stood. In seconds there was a loud *crack*! The rock burst apart, scattering tiny fragments of stone in all directions. Something glittered amidst the rubble. Sure-eyes stepped forward, picked up the sparkling object, and gave it to the prince. It was a diamond larger than a man's fist.

"Well done!" exclaimed the prince. "I shall be pleased to have you join us. But tell me, if your vision is so sharp, how far are we from the Iron Castle?"

Sure-eyes looked off into the distance, but it did not take him very long to reply, "Sir, if you were traveling alone, it should take you at least a year to reach the castle. That is, if you were ever

able to escape this forest. But we three friends shall help you, and with luck, you will be there tonight."

The prince could not resist asking one last question before setting out. "Is there a princess in the castle? Tell me, do you see her?"

"Yes, my lord, I see her. She is asleep. A sorcerer—I see him also—keeps the princess in a high tower. She is guarded by iron bars, and three huge iron bands encircle the outer walls of the castle," answered Sure-eyes.

"You have done well, friend," said the prince

as Sure-eyes replaced his blindfold once more. "It is the sorcerer whom I must face if I am to save the princess." The prince grew grim at the thought of his enemy. "But now, gentlemen, if there are no further companions you would wish me to take into service, I suggest we carry on."

By sundown the travelers had managed to cover an incredible distance by working together to put aside the many obstacles along their path. Now they were coming out of a hollow, climbing steadily up toward the farthest edge of the forest. If they could keep on, escape would soon be within their reach. As they passed through the last ring of tightly knit pines, the heavy tree trunks creaked and groaned, swaying right to left and right again. Pine boughs whispered and brushed their shoulders, though there was no hint of a breeze. Then suddenly they were on the other side of the trees and the Forest of Lost Souls was behind them at last.

Together they stepped out into an open meadow bathed in the fading rosy haze of sunset. For the first time in days the prince breathed a sigh of relief. Now more than ever, he was eager that there be no further delays.

"If we continue to push on, we shall reach the Iron Castle by nightfall," Sure-eyes told the others.

Already they could see the outline of the castle's pointed towers, looming dark and forbidding in the dim twilight. In one of those towers the prin-

cess was held prisoner, thought the prince, and he wanted with all his heart to save her.

"Oh, sir," said Tall. "It looks like a scary place."

"You should know that there is grave danger ahead. I intend to risk my life to free the princess. You three have helped me to find my way out of the forest and I am deeply grateful. But believe me, there is no reason for you to endanger your own lives by following me any farther."

At this, Tall, Large, and Sure-eyes all began to speak at once.

"We wouldn't leave you, sir!"

"We're bound to you, now that we're out of the forest."

"You see, sir," said Tall, finally, "the forest would never have let us go unless we had a reason . . . you, sir . . . when we met you. . . . *You* became our reason. Now we wouldn't dream of leaving you, regardless of the danger. Our destiny is bound to yours." In this they all joined in and fervently agreed.

"All right, then," said the prince, looking at each of them in turn as he shook his head and smiled. "When I set out upon this journey, I must admit I didn't expect company. But I'm proud to have such brave and loyal friends to join me."

So it was settled with a clasp of hands, and they vowed to defeat the sorcerer whatever the cost, or fail together. Then, in the dim light, they traveled on toward the Iron Castle, not knowing what might lie ahead.

Once the castle had been a lively place filled with laughter and the voices of young people, but the sorcerer's curse had seen to all that. On the fateful night he worked his revenge upon the princess, his magic curse floated through the darkened corridors, echoing an evil command: "*From this moment forward be cast into stone.*" Where the words fell the spell took hold. At the same moment, three iron bands coiled about the outer walls, encircling the castle with a serpent's deadly grip.

Then, quite suddenly, in the kitchen, the cat lay still as death before the hearth, the cook sat motionless before her worktable, the fire died, and the small dog busy gnawing on his bone—stopped. In one instant all were turned to stone.

In the castle bedchambers, courtiers tucked in their beds, dreaming of social advancement, stopped their tossing and turning. The ladies-in-waiting, having said good night to their lovely young princess, never guessed that they might never see the dawning light of day again. Yet, so it was, for each and every one in the castle had been turned into smooth white marble.

Outside the castle grounds, the grapes soon withered on the vines. The leaves turned brown and fell to the ground. The grain dried in the fields

and blew away like dust; the grass ceased growing and the flowers failed to bloom that summer or any other.

And so it seemed that the sorcerer had it all his way, if not for one simple fact. While he held the princess in his power, the sorcerer had only managed to capture her human forms, for the princess's spirit, her soul, was still her own.

Legend tells of dreamers whose spirits may travel in other forms. A bird, perhaps, or a butterfly. An owl or a tiny field mouse. A silver wolf or a snow white lamb. And in taking such forms, the spirit of the princess had eluded the sorcerer.

Chapter Four

THAT NIGHT, outside the castle, the disembodied spirits of those who had been turned to stone along with the princess wandered like ghosts with nowhere to go. They drifted aimlessly round and round the castle grounds, waiting . . . hoping for the moment when someone might come to break the spell. Poor spirits, they were the first to spy the small company as they approached.

It was nearly midnight when the prince and his friends crossed the iron drawbridge leading to the gates of the Iron Castle. As they passed through the threshold, the bridge drew itself up behind them and shut with a loud bang.

The inner courtyard led directly to the stables, where the prince put his horse to rest. Other horses were there also, but these animals were all victims of the sorcerer's power. Each one of them stood in its stall, now lifeless stone.

Once within the halls of the castle, the new arrivals saw the result of the sorcerer's work. They crossed from room to room, opening door after door, but every chamber was still and bleak as a tomb. At last they reached the great dining hall. Rows of flaming candles lit the large room. On one wall tall mirrors picked up the flickering candle-light, and within an enormous hearth a roaring fire blazed. In the center of the room a long table was laid with the finest china, silver, crystal, and linen, set for four guests.

Platters of ripe fruit, cheese and fresh bread, savory stew, and wine awaited them. Looking from one to the other, they clearly did not understand if this tasty meal was meant for them, but they were made hungry by the sight. After a few moments, believing their host did not intend to join them, they sat down and began to eat.

When supper was over, the dining hall doors opened of their own accord and a tall figure in long black robes stood in the doorway, coolly regarding them.

It was, of course, the sorcerer. He was a grim sight, standing there. His evil deeds had long since

shaped the contours of his features so that malice and spite, contempt and jealousy were firmly reflected in his sour countenance.

He slowly came forward with the aid of a long staff. Sorcerers live longer than ordinary men and this one in particular, by the look of him, had withstood many winters. Although his hands were gnarled and his long gray beard trailed past his waist, the sorcerer stood like a king before them—a powerful master of his craft. Almost at once the prince noticed the three iron hoops the sorcerer wore around his waist in place of a belt. No doubt, the prince supposed, the visible reminder of the three iron bands which held the castle in his power.

"I know why you're here," said the sorcerer at last. "We shall see if you fare better than the others who have come before you. The conditions are simple enough. But first, you must follow me." Without a further word, he turned and led them out of the hall.

They followed him up a narrow staircase, and at the top he took them into another chamber. They entered a room well lighted by candles. Against the far wall was a large four-poster bed covered in white satin with yards of embroidered lace fastened to a wide canopy that draped the bed on all sides. Behind the lace, lying upon the soft bed, was a white marble statue—it was the princess!

The pale moon hung like a luminous disk outside the arched windows. A breeze ruffled the delicate lace drapes and gently parted the bed-curtains. The prince moved to draw still nearer, hoping to catch a better look, but the sorcerer raised a hand and stopped him.

"As I said, the conditions are quite simple," said the sorcerer. "You can break the spell if on each of the next three nights you can discover what form the princess's spirit takes, even though as you can see I keep her human form within my power. Do it and you will have bested me. *Fail* and you and your companions will meet the fate of all the other

would-be heroes who have tried to challenge me. Believe me, I will be delighted to have you join my gallery of stone statues."

The sorcerer gave them a mock bow and a smile that looked more like a sneer, adding, "If you fear for your lives, you had better leave now while there is still time."

"We accept your challenge," said the prince through clenched teeth.

"Then, gentlemen, I bid you good night." Without another word, the sorcerer swept from the room.

When they were alone, the prince's first thought was the princess, and moving closer, he tried to speak to her. But she neither opened her eyes nor smiled. He knelt down beside the bed, and touching her cold hand, he waited, hoping for the smallest sign of life. Alas, the princess lay motionless upon the white satin bed: a marble statue, no more alive than a piece of beautifully carved stone.

Yet, gazing at her beautiful face, the prince knew he had not been wrong to seek her. Here, indeed, was the maiden he had so often seen in his dreams but had never met in waking life. As he gazed at her, the prince could have wept, for although he had found her at last, the question still remained—could he free her from the sorcerer's curse?

Slowly, his friends came to stand at the foot of the bed. Their eyes filled with tears at the sight of the lovely young princess, still as death, and the prince who loved her so.

"Surely there must be something we can do," said Tall, wiping a tear from his eye. "The night is passing even as we stand here."

"I don't understand the meaning of the challenge," said Large. "After all, the princess is right here, isn't she?"

Tall and Sure-eyes shook their heads no. But it was the prince, coming away from the bed, who explained. "No, Large. Make no mistake, what you see here is only the shell of the princess. She has willed her spirit out of the marble prison the sorcerer has created.

"Even though he holds her human form in his power, the sorcerer has not succeeded in capturing her spirit. If, on each of the next three nights, we can find where her spirit is hiding, we will have beaten the sorcerer and the spell will be broken. That is the challenge he has put before us and we cannot fail or we all are doomed.

"And so, Sure-eyes," said the prince, turning to his sharp-eyed friend. "Can you tell us where the princess has hidden herself tonight?"

Sure-eyes had been waiting for the question. Already he had removed the blindfold from his eyes. Looking around the room, he shook his head and smiled. "We shall find her in none of the obvious places."

Finally he walked to the open window and for a long while remained there, not saying a word. Then, nodding at some distant point that only his keen vision could see, he said, "Yes, I see. I'll not say where exactly, for the sorcerer may be listening. But Tall must take me there or we shall not reach the spot before daybreak."

Then, quietly, so that no one else could hear, he whispered in Tall's ear, "She is a hundred miles off. In the middle of a forest there stands an ancient oak tree. On the very top of the oak there is a single acorn. And it is this tiny acorn that holds the brave spirit of the princess!"

Tall and Sure-eyes started to leave, but the prince wouldn't hear of their going without him. Large agreed to stay behind and keep watch while the others hurriedly departed.

Once outside the castle grounds, Tall hoisted Sure-eyes upon one shoulder and the prince on the other. With the greatest effort, he stretched himself so that in a hundred long strides he managed to reach the ancient oak. High up, so high that only Tall could reach, was the acorn. But they had to hurry—it was nearly dawn and their time was running out.

Just as Tall stretched up, up, up and clasped the precious acorn in his hand, a monstrous dragon appeared before him. Suddenly the terrible creature attacked. But the prince drew his sword and put himself between his friend and the enemy. The dragon breathed fire, scorching trees and earth. With lightning speed, the prince plunged the full length of his sword deep into the dragon's scaly chest. The monster roared more in outrage than in pain. There was a *flash!* And, just as suddenly, the dragon vanished.

"It was the sorcerer all along," said the prince. "Even if he didn't succeed in stealing the acorn, he has managed to delay us. Now, we must be quick, if we have any hope at all of reaching the Iron Castle before daybreak."

Indeed, the sun's golden light was coming up over the horizon. Quickly, Tall took his friends up onto his shoulders and somehow brought them back to the castle, but only just in time.

When they reached the princess's chamber, Large was waiting impatiently. As he was about to ask if they had succeeded, the sorcerer burst into the room.

"Well?" he asked in a gruff voice. "Have you the answer for the first night?"

"We have," answered the prince, and he opened his hand to reveal the acorn.

"Prove it," commanded the sorcerer. This they had not expected to be asked. "Give it here for me to see for myself."

But the prince, thinking quickly, tossed the acorn up into the air as if to throw it to the

sorcerer. In midair the shell burst open, and for an instant the shadowy figure of the princess materialized before disappearing altogether.

CRACK! One of the sorcerer's iron hoops around his waist shattered. *CRACK!* At the same time, an even louder crack was heard as one of the huge iron bands that coiled around the castle was broken.

"We shall see if you fare so well this evening," said the sorcerer as he swept from the room.

Chapter Five

TIME HUNG heavy while they waited. They tried to sleep, but could not; the prince and his friends were far too anxious to rest. Instead they explored the castle, discovering many rich treasures, but all of it was marred by the dismal reminders they saw at every turn, for there were stone statues everywhere they looked; no doubt the countless victims of the sorcerer's cruel power.

In one room they saw a young knight who had been turned into marble in the act of raising his sword to defend himself. It wasn't difficult to guess from whom and why. In another room a similar fate had befallen a knight while running. These were only two of many victims they saw who had failed to win the challenge set for them. The prince and his three friends shuddered to see the frozen forms and each secretly wondered if he, too, would meet with such a horrible fate before too long.

At last, at twilight, supper appeared in the dining hall as it had on the first night—served again by invisible hands. They ate in silence, waiting, and soon nightfall was upon them.

"Will you accept the challenge for a second night?" asked the sorcerer, when he entered the great hall that evening.

"Yes," answered the prince, without hesitation. "Let us begin."

For a second night the sorcerer led the prince and his companions to the princess's chamber and unlocked the door. Allowing them to enter, he nodded in silence and then departed.

The prince went to the princess's bedside and gently touched her hand. There was no change, she was still cold white marble.

"Can you find her for us again tonight?" the prince asked Sure-eyes.

Sure-eyes removed his blindfold and looked out across the countryside. It was a black night, the moon had disappeared behind a wall of thick clouds, and there was not a trace of a star to cast the slightest ray of light. For a few moments, Sure-eyes stood staring in silence.

Finally, he spoke. "Yes, but tonight Large must come with us. I think he'll be needed to accomplish our task."

Refusing to say any more for fear that their words might be carried beyond the room, they hurried out of the castle. Once they believed they were a safe distance away, Sure-eyes told them what he had seen.

"Many hundreds of miles from here, to the west, behind a wall of purple mountains, there lies the vast sea. At the bottom of the sea, there is a bed of oysters. Inside one of those oysters, there is a pearl. Tonight, the spirit of the princess is that *pearl.*"

Somehow Tall managed to carry them all. Each one of his long strides took them many leagues, but even so their time was running short. At last they reached the wall of mountains. The purple rocks towered over them. It would be impossible for Tall even stretched to his fullest to scale such a height.

The sun began to break over the horizon and it seemed this time they were defeated. "Let me try," said Sure-eyes.

In an instant he set himself before the mountains. Concentrating his gaze on one single spot, he pitted his strength against the solid stone. At first nothing happened. But then smoke began to pour from the spot. Suddenly there was a loud explosion and rocks upon rocks fell away. With his powerful gaze, Sure-eyes had succeeded in opening a passage that led right through the mountains and out to the other side. The vast blue sea stood beckoning.

They ran through the tunnel, and when they reached the sea, Sure-eyes pointed to the very spot beneath the waves where they must search. Tall stretched his long arms down, down, down as far as he could, but he could not reach far enough to where the oyster lay.

"It's no good," he shouted back to the others. "I can't reach it. The sea is too deep."

Just then, Large stepped forward. "Wait a moment, my friends," he said matter-of-factly. "I know what must be done."

Blowing himself out, Large began to swell until he was almost as big as the earth. Then he began to drink up the sea. He drank and drank. Soon the water level sank low enough for Tall to reach his arm down to the bottom of the sea.

The others held their breath and waited. Up came Tall's hand out of the sea. He had the oyster in his grasp! Then, with victory so near and no time to spare, a colossal sea monster with arms like an octopus suddenly burst out of the water to seize Tall. It coiled its horrible long tentacles around him and would have the oyster for itself. The prince drew his sword and rushed into the water to save his friend. With each thrust of his sword the prince drove the monster back. But then, the creature's tentacles surrounded him in all directions. The prince hardly knew where to strike first. Blindly he swung his sword left, right, and left again. A scream of

rage issued from the monster, and in a clatter of lightning it vanished so that nothing remained.

Of course they knew without a doubt that it had been the sorcerer and that again he had done his best to delay them. The entire night had passed while they struggled to complete the task. Now, with almost no time left, they had to make their way back to the castle. It was daybreak when they entered the princess's chamber. The sorcerer was waiting.

As though nothing had passed between them that night, he asked, "Well, do you have the answer?" But his eyes blazed with anger.

"Yes," answered the prince, raising up the oyster that held the pearl.

"Prove it, then," demanded the sorcerer.

The prince drew out the precious pearl and held it up in the palm of his hand. When the first ray of sunlight touched the pearl, it melted into thin air. As if through a gossamer veil, the shadowy figure of the princess appeared for an instant before she, too, vanished.

CRACK! Another iron hoop about the waist of the sorcerer shattered. A louder *CRACK!* was heard as the second iron band coiled around the castle snapped apart. In a fury the sorcerer stormed from the room.

The third day dragged by hour by hour; it seemed night would never come. Again they wandered about the castle. They tried to sleep, but could not; there was too much ahead to be at rest.

At sunset, with dinner over, the sorcerer appeared. "Will you take up the challenge for a third and final night?" he asked.

"We accept the challenge," said the prince. "Let us begin at once."

Again the sorcerer led them to the chamber and unlocked the door. But before leaving he told them, "This evening may prove more difficult than the two previous nights. You have one last chance to escape with your lives, or face the consequences of your useless courage."

The prince shook his head, saying, "I'm prepared to risk everything in order to save the princess from your power. But my friends are free to leave, if they so choose."

With one voice, Tall, Large, and Sure-eyes gave a most emphatic no.

"Very well," said the sorcerer. "But mark my words, you will regret your decision." Then he was gone.

When they were alone, the prince went to the princess and studied her face. To his great disappointment nothing had changed—she remained a cold marble statue.

"Tell us, Sure-eyes, where must we seek her tonight?" they all asked.

As he had the last two nights, Sure-eyes removed his ragged blindfold and gazed out the window into the cold dark night. For a very long time he said not a word. The silence was almost too much for them to bear. Large grew so anxious that he said, "Have you gone to sleep, man! Tell us, where is she?"

"I don't know," replied Sure-eyes at last. "I see no sign. No clue. Nothing to guide us."

"Can this be true?" asked Tall in disbelief. "Have we come so far to fail on the *last* night!" As he spoke, his eyelids began to feel so heavy. He yawned. He could barely stay awake. Something was happening to them all.

Sure-eyes and Large began suddenly to nod, to droop. At last they crumpled to the floor as sleep overtook them. The prince struggled to stay awake. He tried desperately to rouse his friends. But it was no use. Tall, Large, and Sure-eyes were in a sleep so deep that nothing could wake them. Finally, the prince could not fight back the strange heaviness he felt. Indeed, he grew so sleepy that his legs gave way from under him, and even before his body slumped to the floor, he was in a deadening sleep.

Of course, it was the sorcerer's work. Seeing that he might lose, he had used magic to tip the scales of fate in his favor. As he had assumed the form of a dragon on the first night and a sea monster on the second, on the third and final night he did more than try to delay them. There was too much at stake to leave anything to chance. Instead, he sent a powerful sleep upon the wings of a gentle breeze, which quickly passed through the open windows of the bedchamber and overcame the prince and his faithful friends.

And so it seemed the game was played out and wickedness would have it all its own way. Night passed, and the spirits imprisoned within the castle walls moaned with regret . . . their freedom would not come about through the efforts of this brave young prince. Alas, he had been their last and best hope.

Chapter Six

A NEW DAY dawned, and with its first light the prince opened his eyes. The sun was breaking through the hazy misty morning, and already he could hear the sorcerer's footsteps as he climbed the stone steps to the chamber. Soon he would be in the room, and they had not discovered the whereabouts of the princess. The third night was over, they had failed, and now they would join the others who had been turned to stone as a result of their failure.

Quickly, the prince tried to wake his friends, but it was too late and he knew it.

The sorcerer opened the door and entered, a cruel smile upon his twisted lips as he looked at them. He tasted revenge and it was sweet indeed.

"Well," he laughed out loud as he asked, "did you pass a successful night?" He waited for the prince to reply.

The others rose up on their feet, trying to shake the heaviness of sleep. Finally, with as much dignity as they could muster, the prince and his three friends stood before the sorcerer.

"Do you have the answer?" demanded the sorcerer.

The prince paused before answering, dreading the moment when he must admit failure. With his hand, he pushed back a lock of hair that had fallen forward across his brow. Finally, he said, "We have not . . ."

Before he could say any more, Sure-eyes quite suddenly interrupted, saying, "Master, it is true, *we have not* had to look very far this time to find the princess. Which is why the sorcerer has found us napping. If you'll allow me, I will continue?"

"By all means," exclaimed the prince, quite bewildered by this new turn of events.

Turning to the sorcerer, Sure-eyes went on, "The princess has placed her spirit in the hands of the prince. She is the *ring* upon his finger. Show him, my lord!"

The prince looked down upon his hands, and there for the first time he saw a ring of splendid beauty upon one of his fingers. It had not been there the night before or ever before for that matter. He pulled off the ring and tossed it into the air as the sorcerer commanded, "Prove that what you say is true! *Or forever be cast into stone!*"

For a split second the ring hung in midair, then it vanished and the spirit of the princess appeared like a beam of light. It drifted to her marble figure, resting on the bed and bathing the smooth white stone with shining light.

CRACK! The third hoop around the sorcerer's waist shattered. *CRACK!* The final iron band holding the castle in its evil grasp snapped. There was a great clatter of thunder and a rumble and a roar. The castle trembled to its very foundation. With a scream of outrage, the sorcerer transformed himself

into a huge black bird. Spreading its wings, the creature flew out the window. It was never seen again, for the spell cast over the Iron Castle was broken forever.

The princess took hold of the prince's hand as he moved to help her rise from her bed. Indeed, she was flesh and blood once more. At first, our prince could only stare at her with love and wonder, for words to match his happiness seemed utterly inadequate.

Tall, Large, and Sure-eyes shyly came forward and bowed low before her. She gave them each a glowing smile and kissed their foreheads, which made them blush with pleasure.

"Thank you, all of you," she said, "for helping to free me from the sorcerer's binding spell."

Then, turning to the prince, she continued. "You and your companions must choose what reward you wish. My kingdom and my fate are in your hands. We owe you a great debt for rescuing us."

At last, the prince could find words to speak of what was in his heart. "Your Royal Highness, I ask for nothing but your love—to give or to withhold, it is your choice alone."

The princess looked long into the prince's eyes and smiled. "You had my love even before you arrived at my castle, for I have dreamed of loving you."

"And I of you, princess," he told her as he

took her hands in his and gently kissed them.

There was the most splendid celebration you can imagine. The lords and ladies awoke and began to shout with gladness. One courtier after another yawned, tossed off his coverlet, and pinched himself to make certain he was truly there. In the kitchen the servants stretched, and leaping to their feet, they began to dance for joy. The little dog woke up and resumed chewing on his bone. Another dog licked his master, and the cats licked their paws while they purred with pleasure. The horses neighed in their stalls and twitched their tails. Birds perched upon windowsills, singing sweet songs, and fish jumped in the swiftly flowing stream. The grass began to grow, flowers bloomed, and the trees spread their branches and sprouted new leaves. The magic spell was broken, and life with all its sounds and smells and motion had returned to the castle once more.

Rockets were set off from the tallest parapets. Great bursts of colored fireworks flamed and exploded, shooting brilliant light across the sky and finally came showering down with an array of giant stars, birds, and even a dragon, which admittedly gave Tall, Large, and Sure-eyes a start. "It's certainly a good likeness," remarked Tall.

The knights and noblemen came to give homage to the prince in gratitude for their deliverance. But the prince pointed instead to his three friends, saying, "There are the gentlemen to thank, and not me. When I took them into my service, I never knew how helpful they would be. No doubt, for all my efforts, I, too, would have ended up as another of the sorcerer's statues, if not for their bravery and skill."

Chapter Seven

AFTER DAYS and days of the jolliest merrymaking, the prince and the princess, accompanied by their three faithful friends, set out for the prince's homeland.

The old king wept for joy at the sight of the young couple. There was, of course, a spectacular wedding and everyone from both kingdoms managed to attend. After the ceremony, the king wished to bestow a great fortune upon the three friends who had done so much to help his son. And the prince and the princess begged them to share their kingdoms.

Tall, Large, and Sure-eyes smiled, shook their heads, and said no. "You have taught us something

more valuable than riches could ever give us," said Tall.

"It's true," Large agreed. "While we wandered alone in the Forest of Lost Souls, we thought of ourselves as useless misfits, no good to anyone, not even ourselves."

"Outcasts," said Sure-eyes, who no longer wore his ragged blindfold to hide his sharp eyes. "But you gave us a chance to prove ourselves. And to learn that being different might mean being better. Instead of being ashamed, we've learned to be proud."

"And bold," interjected Tall with a laugh.

"And brave," added Large, smiling broadly.

"So we're going to try to continue to be useful," Tall said, finally. "In fact, we've decided to join forces. Together, we'll travel across the land and perhaps our unique skills will come in handy. Who knows, one day our feats might even be legendary!"

That is exactly what came to pass, and for all anyone knows, Tall, Large, and Sure-eyes are about their noble business to this very day.